THE DOG WHO GREW TOO MUCH

WRITTEN AND ILLUSTRATED
BY POLLY CAMERON

COWARD-McCANN, INC NEW YORK

je
c.5

Library of Congress Catalog Card Number: 58-10184

MANUFACTURED IN THE UNITED STATES OF AMERICA

ALSO BY POLLY CAMERON

THE CAT WHO THOUGHT HE WAS A TIGER

THE CAT WHO COULDN'T PURR

Fred lived in a small apartment in New York City.
He was lonely and wanted a little dog to keep him company.

He went to a pet shop and chose a two-month-old puppy named Stilt.

Fred played with Stilt in the morning before he went to work.
He played with her at night when he came home. He was very happy.

Stilt was happy, too. She walked around on all the furniture
while Fred was away.

When Stilt was three months old, Fred came home and found her stuck under the couch. She had gained fifteen pounds in one month.

When Stilt was four months old, she had gained another fifteen pounds. Fred couldn't push her collar past her ears. He bought her a larger collar.

Stilt's nose stuck in her dinner bowl. Fred bought her a bigger bowl.

When Stilt was five months old, she was too big for her bed.
She slept in Fred's bed. Fred slept on the couch.

Stilt's favorite trick was to push the bed against the door.
When Fred came home from work he had to climb in the window.

When Stilt was six months old, she chewed up all her toys.
Fred bought her a football.

Stilt played football every day. When Fred came home all the
furniture was tipped over. Fred was not very happy.

Fred's neighbors were not happy either. When they heard
Stilt moving furniture they thought it was an earthquake.
When she barked they thought it was a lion.

Fred's neighbors and his landlord came to see him. "Fred," they said,
"either Stilt leaves the apartment or you leave the apartment."

Fred had no choice. He moved to another apartment with a big garden. Stilt could play in the garden without knocking over any furniture.

When Fred came home from work he played football with Stilt.
He learned to duck when Stilt jumped at him.

Stilt grew bigger and bigger. She learned a new game.
She dug caves in the garden with long tunnels joining the caves.

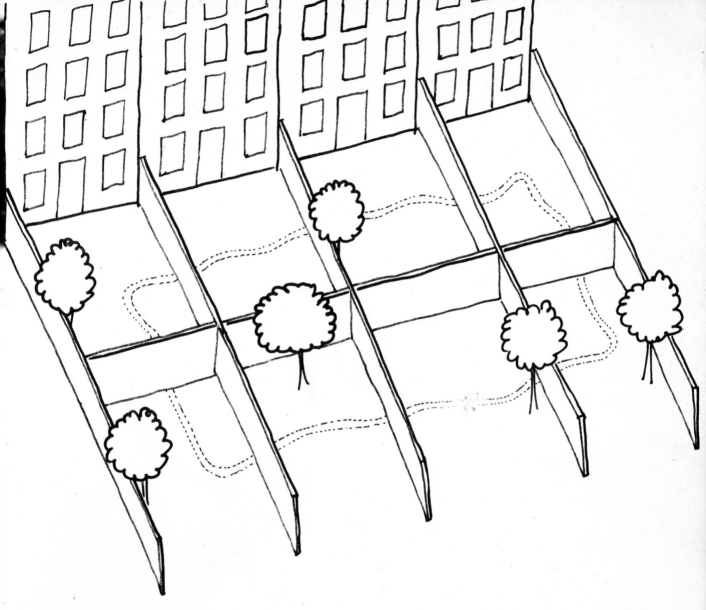

She dug a tunnel under the fence and right through
to all the gardens in the block.

She dug a tunnel right out into the street.

People were frightened when they saw this giant dog trotting down the street. They ran inside stores and hid.

Stilt leaned against a butcher shop window. The window crashed in. Stilt grabbed a mouthful of sausages.

Two policemen rode up on horseback to see what was happening. Stilt was pleased to see two big horses and she wanted to play.

The horses reared back in fright and galloped away.
Stilt galloped happily after them.

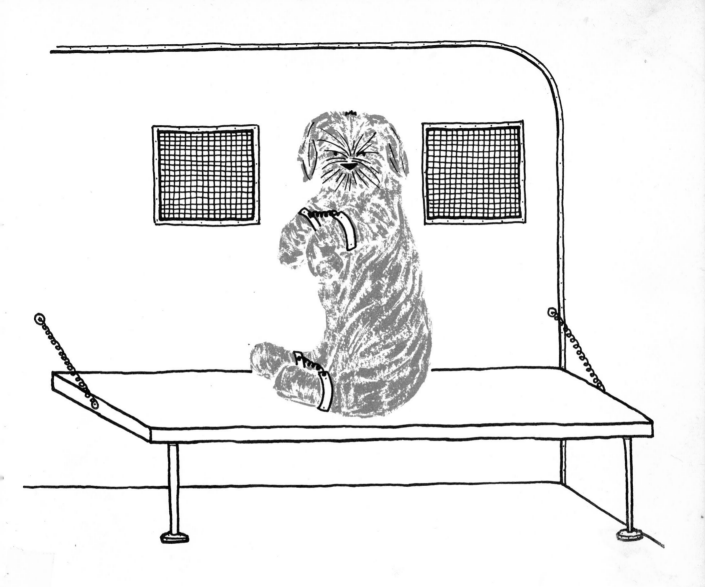

It took the police force and the fire department to catch Stilt.
They put two pairs of handcuffs on her feet and drove her home.

"Fred," they said, "either Stilt leaves the city or you leave the city."

Fred had no choice. He moved to a ranch in Arizona.
There were no people on the ranch for Stilt to bother.

Stilt had a fine time. She played with the horses and herded the sheep.

She chased the cows into the barn at milking time.

Stilt worked hard on the ranch. "At last," Fred said,
"Stilt will not get into any more trouble."

One day Fred heard strange noises in the barn. He climbed
up to the hayloft to see what they were.

There was Stilt, smiling proudly down at eleven little puppies.

When the puppies were one month old,
they used Stilt as a playground.

When the puppies were two months old,
they played catch with the eggs in the henyard.

When the puppies were three months old,
they played a new game called Fight.

But Fred didn't care and Stilt didn't care.